carte blanche

greetings ltd ®

© 2008 Carte Blanche Greetings Ltd ®

www.carteblanchegreetings.com

First edition for the United States published in 2010 by Barron's Educational Series, Inc.

First published in the U.K. by HarperCollins Children's Books in 2008 under the title:
Me to You—With Love at Christmas.

The Me to You oval, Tatty Teddy signature, and bear logo are all registered trademarks of Carte Blanche Greetings Ltd.
© Carte Blanche Greetings Ltd ® P.O. Box 500, Chichester, PO20 2XZ, U.K.

All inquiries should be addressed to:
Barron's Educational Series, Inc.
250 Wireless Boulevard
Hauppauge, NY 11788
www.barronseduc.com

ISBN-13: 978-0-7641-6343-2
ISBN-10: 0-7641-6343-4

Printed in China

9 8 7 6 5 4 3 2 1

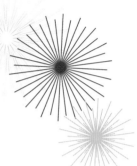

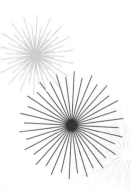

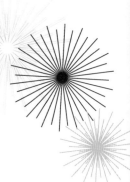

Celebrate Christmas with the people you love.

You make
my heart jingle.

Christmas is a time
for caring and sharing.

You are the
icing on my
Christmas cake!

You make
Christmastime special.

A time to share
happy moments.

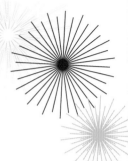

Love is the
greatest gift of all!

You make all my
dreams come true.

You are
my Christmas star!

The best thing
about Christmas is
spending time with you.

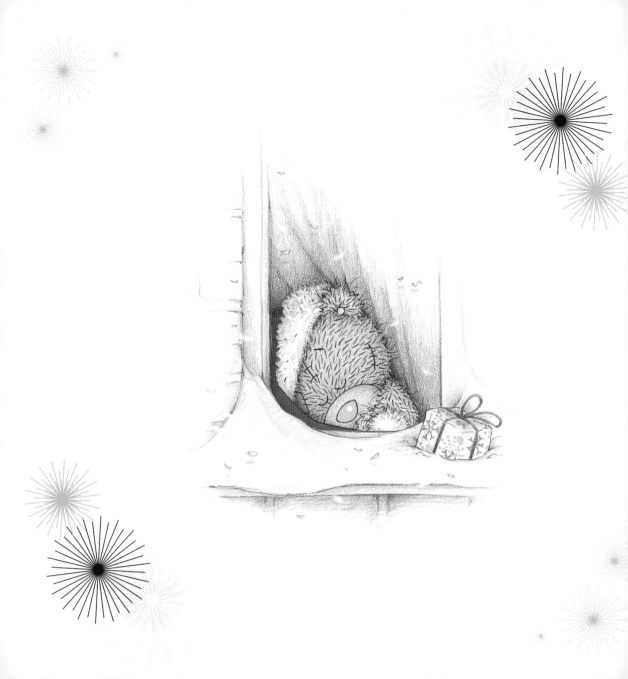

Wishing you all
my love at Christmastime.